The Three Little Tamales is the story of "The Three Little Pigs" with a Mexican flavor. Readers who enjoyed my earlier book, *The Runaway Tortilla*, wrote to me asking for another story about the tortilla. I pointed out that I couldn't do that, since Señor Coyote ate her in the end. "Write about something else," they suggested. I went to Catalina's, my favorite Mexican restaurant, and looked at the menu. What else could I write about? Tamales, of course! —E.A.K.

GLOSSARY

Casita (ca-SEE-ta): A little house, cabin.

Fiesta (fee-ESS-ta): Party, celebration, holiday.

Guapo (GWAH-po): Handsome.

Laredo (La-RAY-do): A city in Texas.

Lindo (LEEN-do): Lovely.

Lobo (LOH-bo): Wolf.

Muy (MWEE): Very.

Por favor (POHR fah-BOHR): Please.

Señor (Seh-NYOR): Mister.

Señorita (Seh-nyo-REE-tah): Miss.

Tamale (tah-MAH-lay): Cornmeal dough mixed with meat and chili peppers, wrapped in cornhusks, and steamed.

Taqueria (tah-kay-REE-ah): A small restaurant.

Tía (TEE-ah): Aunt.

Tío (TEE-oh): Uncle.

Tonto (TOHN-to): Foolish.

Tortilla (tor-TEE-yah): Mexican flatbread.

Marshall Cavendish Corporation, 99 White Plains Road, Tarrytown, NY 10591
www.marshallcavendish.us/kids

Library of Congress Cataloging-in-Publication Data
Kimmel, Eric A.
  The three little tamales / by Eric A. Kimmel ; illustrated by Valeria Docampo.
  p. cm.
  Summary: In this variation of "The Three Little Pigs" set in the Southwest, three little tamales escape from a restaurant before they can be eaten, and set up homes in the prairie, cornfield, and desert.
  ISBN 978-0-7614-5519-6
  [1. Fairy tales. 2. Tamales—Fiction. 3. Wolves—Fiction.] I. Docampo, Valeria, 1976- ill. II. Title.
  PZS.K527Tgp 2009
  [E]—dc22
200S01073S
The illustrations are rendered in oil on paper.
Book design by Becky Terhune
Editor: Margery Cuyler

Printed in China
First edition

1 3 5 6 4 2

Marshall Cavendish
Children

The Three Little Tamales

by **Eric A. Kimmel** • illustrated by **Valeria Docampo**

Marshall Cavendish Children

Once upon a time in Texas there lived a couple known to all as Tío José and Tía Lupe. Tío José and Tía Lupe owned a *taquería*, a little restaurant. Everyone said that Tía Lupe made the best tortillas and tamales in all of Texas.

Every morning she wrapped the tamales in cornhusks and steamed them in a pot. When they were done, she put them by the window to cool.

One day, three little tamales saw a tortilla rolling by.

"Where are you going?" they asked the tortilla.

"I'm running away," the tortilla told them. "If I stay here, someone's going to eat me. You'll be eaten, too. You'd better run!"

"We don't want to be eaten," the three little tamales said. They decided to run away together. They jumped out the window and ran down the road before anyone knew they were gone.

The first little tamale ran until she came to the prairie. She breathed in the smell of sagebrush.

"I want to live here," the first little tamale said.

She built herself a little house, a *casita*, out of sagebrush and moved in. She went to sleep that night surrounded by the sweet smell of sage.

The second little tamale ran until he
came to a cornfield. He listened to the
rustling cornstalks.

"That sounds like music. I want to
live here," the second little tamale said.

He built his *casita* out of cornstalks
and moved in. He went to sleep that night
listening to the music of cornstalks.

The third little tamale ran until she came to the desert. She saw cactus bristling with thorns.

"Cactus will make a strong house. The thorns will protect me," the third little tamale said.

She built her *casita* out of tough, prickly cactus and moved in. She slept soundly that night, protected by cactus.

The three little tamales
lived happily for a time. Then
one day who should come
trotting by but Señor Lobo,
the Big Bad Wolf. The first
little tamale saw him coming.
She ran inside her sagebrush
house and shut the door.

Señor Lobo walked up to the house.
He looked in the window and said,
Señorita Tamale,
por favor,
I want to come in,
so open the door.

The first little tamale replied,
Señor Lobo, muy lindo,
I'm sorry to say,
I won't let you in,
so please go away.

Señor Lobo answered,
I'll huff and I'll puff
like a Texas tornado
and blow your casita
from here to Laredo!

Then he huffed and puffed until he blew the
sagebrush *casita* to pieces. But the first little
tamale got out just in time. She ran to her
brother's house, the one made of cornstalks.

The second little tamale saw her coming.
He opened the door and let her in, just as
Señor Lobo arrived.

Señor Lobo walked up to
the cornstalk house.
He looked in the window
and said,
  Señor Tamale,
  por favor,
  I want to come in,
  so open the door.

The second little
tamale replied,
  Señor Lobo, muy guapo,
  I'm sorry to say,
  I won't let you in,
  so please go away.

Señor Lobo answered,
  I'll huff and I'll puff
  like a Texas tornado
  and blow your casita
  from here to Laredo!

Then he huffed and puffed until he
blew the cornstalk *casita* to pieces.
But the two little tamales escaped
just in time. They ran to their
sister's house in the desert, the
one made of cactus.

The third little tamale saw them
coming. She opened the door and let
them in, just as Señor Lobo arrived.
   Señor Lobo walked up to the
cactus house. He looked in the
window. He knocked on the door.
"OW!" he yelled as the cactus
thorns stuck him. Then he said,
   Señorita Tamale,
   por favor,
   I want to come in,
   so open the door.

The third little tamale replied,
Señor Lobo, muy tonto,
I'm sorry to say,
I won't let you in,
so please go away.

Señor Lobo answered,
I'll huff and I'll puff
like a Texas tornado
and blow your casita
from here to Laredo!

"Go ahead and try. I don't think you can," the third little tamale told him. That made Señor Lobo angry. He huffed and he puffed . . . and he huffed and he puffed. He huffed and puffed until he was out of breath. But the little *casita* never budged because the cactus was tough, its roots were strong, and its long, sharp thorns were woven tightly together.

"I know what I'll do," Señor Lobo said. "If I can't blow this house to pieces, I'll climb down the chimney. The three little tamales will never know I'm coming."

But when Señor Lobo climbed on top of the house, the cactus thorns pricked his paws. "Ay! Ay! Ay!" he yelped as he tiptoed across the roof.

"Señor Lobo is on the roof! He is coming down the chimney! What will we do? We'd better run!" cried the first little tamale.

"We'd better hide!" said the second little tamale.

"No, we won't!" said the third little tamale. "I'm not afraid of Señor Lobo. I know a better way to deal with him than running away and hiding." She told the others her plan. They agreed to help her.

The three little tamales filled a pot with water and set it on the fire to boil. They heard Señor Lobo climbing down the chimney.

"Ay! Ay! AAAYYYYY!!!!" he yelled.

SPLASH! He fell into the pot of water. CLANG! The three little tamales covered the pot with an iron lid.

"Let me out!" Señor Lobo howled.

"No, we can't," the three little tamales replied. "We're cooking wolf tamales for dinner."

"I don't want to be a tamale!" Señor Lobo
yelled. He jumped out of the pot, climbed
back up the chimney, and ran across the
roof. He didn't let the cactus thorns slow
him down. He ran until he was out of
sight. And he never came back.

Señor Lobo was gone for good. The three little tamales never had to worry about him again. So they had a fiesta and invited all their friends to celebrate.

And who were the friends who came to the fiesta of the three little tamales?

Why, the runaway tortillas, of course!